Fall of a Bride

Soul Calling

AF520632

notionpress.com

Fall of a Bride

Soul Calling

NOUSH

notionpress.com

Notion Press

Old No. 38, New No. 6
McNichols Road, Chetpet
Chennai - 600 031

First Published by Notion Press 2016
Copyright © Noush 2016
All Rights Reserved.

ISBN 978-93-86073-29-7

This book has been published with all efforts taken to make the material error-free after the consent of the author. However, the author and the publisher do not assume and hereby disclaim any liability to any party for any loss, damage, or disruption caused by errors or omissions, whether such errors or omissions result from negligence, accident, or any other cause.

No part of this book may be used, reproduced in any manner whatsoever without written permission from the author, except in the case of brief quotations embodied in critical articles and reviews.

For Koohoo, 3 Aces and Sun

Acknowledgements

You can only bloom if your soil provides you anchorage. This one's for my grandpa A.N Chanchal who has always been a source of inspiration, my grandma who gave all her time and patience to my myriads of gibberish talks. Both of you are dearly missed.

My daughter Shubhrita (Koohoo), for writing me cards of 'Best Mommy' and encouraging me to love what I do. My husband Sunny, who has been rock of Gibraltar for me and for giving me the insight of giving words to my expressions.

For mom and dad who gave me a platform to surface my talent up. Amrita and Aashna; my beautiful sisters for pampering me to write my heart out.

My in-laws who palliated my burden while I was busy writing my book.

Ruchi, my soul sister who since childhood has always appreciated every piece of writing, said to be mine. Huda Hyder, who has helped me tons with the editing and treated me at various food joints across Jaipur.

This one's also for all those who after reading this piece of writing will bring about a change in their lives and rise and shine.

Noush

Chapter 1

'Can I be your novel… Can I paint you pink…can you
fall on me my angel…only for today can we sin…'
she woke up to this song echoing in the remotest
parts of her brain, bringing her back to life.

"You shouldn't put yourself under so much of strain. Lie down, comm'on be a brave woman, lie down." She was on the hospital bed and the nurse was trying to mollycoddle her back to that bizarre bed which wasn't even her favourite colour!

"Doctor, the patient is out of coma." The lady clad up in white creased uniform sprinted across the cubicle to bring in the doc.

"Doctor, the patient is out of coma," she reiterated.

For how long have I been here? What happened to me? Oh God!!! The pain is ascending…but…but… Why am I still alive…? And she wandered away into infinite oblivion.

Pacing in emotional vehemence in the waiting alley of the hospital, was a strong and sturdy grey haired man who was in possession of deep penetrating eyes, dominant chin, sharp straight nose and full lips. His forehead bore etched out impressions of experience and exasperation.

Where did he go wrong? Was he too over protective…was he never around when she needed him the most…was she paying for his sins…must be! These questions were bombing his very existence as a Father.

"Hello, is this Mr. Singha?"

"Yes. Who is it?"

"Is Sayra your daughter?"

"Who is it?"

"Is Sayra your daughter?"

"Yes, she is. What is it about?"

"This is Michael Jacob from Irwin Road Police Station. Sayra is in critical condition. She has been taken to Winscent Margo Hospital, Debbing Road."

"Mr. Ja… Mr. Jacob. This is Sayra's father. What happened to her? Is she all right? Good Lord! Is my child alright?" He stood embalmed.

"Mr. Singha kindly reach the hospital as soon as you can, Sayra is in the ICU. Goodbye."

He instantly felt giddy. He knew it from the beginning - he should not have given in to Sayra's persistent pleadings of getting married to Amol, her childhood friend. Amol, the scoundrel.

Sayra was thrown by her tyrant destiny into the state of being the only girl child of a single parent-her short tempered father. Her mother divorced Rijoy for the same reasons. In addition to being aggressive, he was insecure and suspicious and used to doubt Poonam's character too.

He not only inflicted her physically but, also battered her soul. Poonam decided to leave Rijoy when Sayra was 7; being financially infirm, she could not get Sayra's custody and with a heavy heart had to leave her with Rijoy who possessed all the qualities of a sterling father and loved his daughter more than his ego.

Poonam now runs a lifestyle brand 'Moksha'. She worked her finger to bone to bring it to eminence but could never muster up her courage to face Rijoy and meet her darling angel Sayra. She had everything she wanted in her life, but a family and most importantly her lifeline -her daughter.

Chapter 2

Rijoy was born to a happily married couple who died in a car accident when Rijoy was 13 years of age. He was left at the mercy of his not so loving uncle and aunt, who mauled his soul. It was when wrath and anger started proliferating in his mind and demeanor, but could not affect the mellowness of his heart. He became a tough nut soft to the core. The period of adolescence when he needed someone's guiding hand the most, he suffered verbal and physical abuses thrust upon him by his foster parents. He felt miserable and the more he was drawn into self pity the more hideous he grew inside out.

He failed classes more often than pass.

He failed his tenth boards for the second time…and no one was bothered. He was made to repeat class X with his junior batches. Rijoy had turned into a rambunctious fellow scaring the wits out of everyone but, Poonam. Poonam was the most beautiful and the most intelligent girl of the class who did not react to Rijoy's emphatic anger. She was a girl of strong conviction and she knew that anger is the sign of inner weakness. Poonam sympathized with Rijoy moreover.

It was the ingress of pleasant winters. And one fine day Rijoy could not complete his Mathematics assignment hence, was awarded the punishment to stay back after school and not leave until the submission. He didn't mind staying back at the school the whole day as it wouldn't have made much difference; he had no home to return to, just a house full of intense dislike and negligence for him which would have been more than happy not to hear his footsteps. Poonam didn't take long to realize that solving Mathematics problem was a tough row to hoe for Rijoy and she chose to stay back to help him. That was the inception of their love in their hearts. Poonam started staying back for half an hour after school to help Rijoy in studies. Days passed and then months. A task that was taken up as an act of kindness turned into something more beautiful.

Poonam could feel her growing inclination towards Rijoy turn into love. She was the first one after Rijoy's parents to have known his softer side. Rijoy was also drawn towards Poonam for the same reason. She had become his invincible strength. Rijoy could feel his anger descend and love take over his heart which now resonated with Poonam's name.

The class X results were soon to be declared and Poonam was more anxious than Rijoy. It was a balmy summer morning and Poonam was dreaming of Rijoy when her father dashed into her room to announce her result. She had again topped the class, but seemed puzzled as if not in a mood to celebrate her success.

"Poonam, you did it again... You made it to the merit... Poonam... You always do us proud."

But Poonam wanted to listen to Rijoy's success story.

"Oh yes, thanks dad. Can I see the paper?" She asked for the paper stoically.

Her dad handed over the newspaper to her; surprised at her behaviour.

Roll no. 1656, 1658, 1662…1667. It was right there, Rijoy's roll number was right there. Roll no 1667! She jumped in joy and elation.

"I love you, I love you, and I love you so much dad… oh am so happy, so happy, and so very happy." She was dancing and singing, she was on seventh heaven. Rijoy not only did pass but also scored first division. Her love had brought colours…she was…no **they were a success together**.

There was no looking back from then on for both of them. Rijoy and Poonam pursued Engineering together from the same college and were famously known as 'the beauty and the brawn', inseparable from each other. Life was smiling at them and Poonam's parents had no objection to their relationship; on the other hand Rijoy's uncle and aunt didn't really bother much.

As destiny favoured them, both were recruited by the same MNC for the same position and soon after they were tied in the sacred bond of marriage. Rijoy rented a flat and both of them shifted away from sorrows and grievances into a love nest of their own, to celebrate their wedlock.

That was the beginning of the story…the real story of 'the beauty and the brawn'.

Chapter 3

They had kissed earlier but today was the night which was going to bring out the intensity of their love that they had nurtured in their hearts from their age of teens.

Poonam sat curled up on the bed wearing a rose red heavily embroidered lehenga weaved in ethnic art. The blouse had a thin strap at the back exposing more of her bare and beautiful skin. A flimsy veil covered her face, hiding her shyness from the world and her world was now Rijoy. The room was dimly lit but the resplendence of her beauty had illuminated all the corners of the room.

She saw a silhouetted figure on the marble floor where the iridescence of her youth was scattered. Her heart skipped a beat. It was Rijoy…her Rijoy. Rijoy who owned her and the beauty with all her heart and soul wanted to be his proud possession.

Rijoy was carrying a box wrapped in glittering hearts and presented it to his lucky charm.

"Wha…what is it?" Her voice trembled with joy and anxiety both.

"It's a surprise, a naughty surprise." His eyes sparkled with mischief to lighten her weighed spirit…weighed with the unknown sequence of the eventful night.

She laughed softly and the tinkling sound of her vivacious laughter filled the room with colour and exuberance.

"If the gift is naughty then let me be naughtier." She said obliterating her coyness.

"The naughty bride and the haughty groom… Mmm sounds great!"

"That sounds rude Rijoy. Haughty and that I won't let you be. You will forever remain my love wouldn't you Rij?"

"Show me your love first tigress."

"Let me see the present first my demanding tiger." She teased Rijoy by moving away from him towards the gift box.

It was a see-through negligee woven in shades of black and wine-the colours of sin…permitted sin in the darkness of night. The colour of her cheeks rose to pink, then red and then to the colours of love. She closed herself in the bathroom to quickly slip out of her wedding dress and slip into the naughtiness of night.

Rijoy desperately awaited the advent of his beautiful bride garbed in his desire of love. And as the rainbow appears after a soft shower of rain; Poonam covered in her impeccable youth stepped out both of the bathroom and pink shyness. Rijoy was spellbound, under the spell of her charm, her beauty and her nakedness.

"The present is naughty indeed!"

“The present isn’t as naughty as your husband is,” said Rijoy pulling the raw uncovered Poonam towards him.

Poonam fell in his arms first and then on the bed. They kissed as they had never kissed before, their tongues entangled, trying to overpower each other. Rijoy slipped his hand under her negligee gripping her soft mounts with his strong grip. He squeezed, she winced, he squeezed more and she was ecstatic. His wild mouth now moved towards her pink domed milky white, soft but firm mounts. Poonam had surrendered to the obstinate demands of his love making and was transported to a land of passion and wildness.

His hands moved from her mounts to her inner folded depressions. She moaned in pleasure and kissed him harder. He withdrew himself from her embrace and moved down to lick the hot and wet sweetness dripping out. She was euphoric, her perfect round hips moved with his flickering tongue up and down in a sensuous move. He now stood up to unveil his muscular strength unzipping the fly of his pants and entered into the world of deep dark pleasure and love. She groaned in pain and then enjoyed the pain to the core.

“Don’t stop Rijoy, just don’t stop…”

He moved in and out and then deeper and deeper till he flooded her with the stream of his love. They fell into each other’s arms to sleep peacefully for the rest of the night.

The next morning it was Rijoy who got up first to prepare tea and breakfast for Poonam.

"Good morning Mrs. Singha," he said planting a warm kiss on her cheeks.

Mrs. Singha... Mrs. Poonam Singha...how often had she enunciated her name like this and every time she pronounced it out aloud she had goosebumps. Now it sounded so surreal that she flowed with the magical words, Rijoy had to bring her back to reality by dipping her index finger in the less hot tea than her.

"Ouch! Rijoy!" She immediately sucked her finger into her warm and wet mouth. She looked so divine that Rijoy forgot the scrambled eggs and pancakes that he had prepared for his wife and slipped into the bed to make passionate love to her. It was more passionate than the night before.

It was now time for the love birds to leave their nest and fly to their office, together...and they loved it.

Poonam was brilliant and it was a known fact. She was a far more efficient employee than her husband. The Management decided to give Poonam a raise and to add icing on the cake, a promotion too and that too within 6 months. That meant that she would be heading a team of 12 executives under her and Rijoy was one out of the lot.

They both celebrated her success at 'The Art Cafe' and feasted on cold cut Russian salad, sweet corn chicken soup and chicken stick on sizzler.

They enjoyed their dinner and when it came to pay the bill, Poonam called it her treat and advanced the payment to the Manager. ***First blow to the male ego!***

She was complimented time and again by her bosses for meeting the targets on time and planning out new strategies which worked miracles for the company. She couldn't savor the fruit of her continuous triumphs for she only knew what it was to hold sway over a frustrated husband and make him work.

One day Rijoy asked, "What is it that you wear on your skin that makes you glow day by day?"

She answered, "Confidence!"

The beauty was a proficient Head and the brawn was a muscular brain. She dominated in the office with her wits and he at home in the skin of her man. She had a reason and his reason was sheer revenge. The nest once made up of fresh green twigs was now drying into sharp bleeding thorns. Their love making from becoming less passionate day by day was now reduced to them being slaves to their lust.

Rijoy now eyed Poonam with suspicion and doubted her capabilities. She was accused of fostering illegitimate relationships with her bosses. That was the only way he could reason her success in her profession and torture her mentally every day. This had become a matter of daily mundane and Rijoy got used to misbehaving to such an extent that the place where he used to plant warm passionate kisses he impressed upon his five ugly muscular fingers; blatant enough to apologize.

Not only was Poonam in physical pain but she had received the blow deep down in her heart that made the already shattered love castle turn into rubbles.

Chapter 4

Sayra had shown no signs of improvements on the following days. The doctors were trying to bring her back to life and the cops were prodding her past.

Amol was in Chicago, the city of his dreams away from the dream girl he thought he loved. Amol and Sayra had decided to call their marriage off as neither of them was able to take more of it.

Amol never had imagined that his love story will come to a climax like this (little did he realize that it wasn't love, it was his lust story). Sayra was a stupid girl she must have known that she could not own Amol and let alone own she didn't even have the right to interfere into his relationships with other girls. After all, they were living in the modern era and he well deserved his space. Once he had also offered Sayra the proposal of open marriage and furthermore they could have shifted to Chicago and enjoyed the life of bliss; he was doing her a favour. But that dumb wit created a fuss out of the entire issue. He definitely wasn't anyone's property and possessed all the rights to live it the way he wanted.

She called it uncouth of him to make advances on other girls after marriage. 'Uncivilized', yes uncivilized was the word that she used for him. It wasn't his fault solely to be one of such kinds, she was equally responsible, for she couldn't hold him back. And on the top of that, his parents were also not happy with Sayra. Not to forget, Sayra's father, Rijoy Singha who was the root cause of their broken marriage.

Lost in his reverie, he forgot that he was driving a car. He had to bring his car to a sudden halt when about to bump into a postbox.

He cursed Sayra for this incident as well, if only she could have kept him happy he would not have wandered away from her. He held her responsible for his vagrancy.

He heard the ringing of his phone just then.

"Amol, Amol this is Rijoy."

He was about to disconnect.

"Amol, Sayra met with an accident. She is in coma."

"Uncle…"…long silence.

Rijoy was apprehensive about his response. He was talking to Amol after 2 years; their relationship was not a pleasant one. Amol had also imposed restrictions on Sayra from meeting her Dad for he held him responsible for all the mishaps of his married life.

Amol didn't know how to react as they were anyhow going to end their marriage soon. But for the sake of their friendship that lasted till their wedding; his conscience ingrained with catharsis compelled him to show his concern.

"Amol, can you hear me?"

"Yes, I can hear you. How did that happen?"

"We all are clueless here. She must have been driving rashly on the hills. Sayra was found badly injured in the trench and the car all in ashes."

Amol felt as if his heart had stopped beating.

After much effort he spoke, "How is she now?"

"She is in coma; no bone in her body is left intact. Doctors too fear whether she is going to make it or not. Amol… Amol I have lost her once and I don't want to lose her again," drowned in emotions he was finding it difficult to speak. "How soon can you come back to India?"

"By the next flight." They hung up.

He had no control over his emotions. Tears trickled down his unshaven jaw leaving a trail of memories behind it. He wanted to rush to Sayra immediately and wanted to take her in his arms and tell her that he loved her and wanted her back…he had been so unkind to her…tell her that he is going to change… **No he has changed!**

Sayra was waiting for a miracle to change Amol and bring him back to her. Now the miracle had happened. But at the cost of…

Chapter 5

Rijoy was broken deep inside but, not for the very first time. His entire world crashed once again. He somehow survived without Poonam because he had his sweet little daughter by his side and he had decided to give Poonam's share of love to Sayra.

He could no more handle his accursed life, he felt as if he had grown too old in the past few days. He was desperately waiting for Amol's arrival. He had not disclosed it to Amol that not only was he called to visit Poonam but also for investigation. The police was suspecting it to be a case of not only rash driving but a different connotation to it was, an attempt to commit **SUICIDE**.

Rijoy was restless. He was finding it difficult to sleep. Syara would have been sleeping peacefully, but he so much wanted her to wake up from this deep slumber. He reached for the switch and turned his computer on. He knew what he was going to do. His hands trembled, he hesitated for a while but with quivering hands he typed the letters on the search engine.

M…O…K…S…H…A… POONAM… ENTER

Whether she still writes Singha or not…

Moksha- jewellery brand, Poonam Sehdev

Moksha Tiles- no Poonam

Moksha spa- no Poonam

Moksha- your own lifestyle brand- Poonam Singha

Poonam Singha...so she still writes my name.

Contact: 91-084-345-621

This is the landline number of her store. Should I call... should I not. Not, it is already half past midnight. I will make a call at 10 am tomorrow; the store will be functioning by then.

He popped in two sleeping pills and slept.

He woke up to his morning alarm. It was 6 in the morning. He took a bath and dressed himself in Poonam's favourite colour, a black shirt which still fitted him after 18 years to his wonder. He had lost his appetite after what had happened to Sayra. His infirmity battled with his courage and reflected on his skin which had lost its colour and shine. He looked blanched.

He was going to do today what he hadn't done in the past 14 years... Speak to Poonam...his wife...his ex wife, but still his love... Mrs Poonam Singha. She still wrote his name with hers.

91-084-345-621

He dialed these numbers on his mobile waiting to hear Poonam's voice after two years.

Yes, two years. He often used to make blank calls to Poonam on her mobile from various public phone booths to ensure that she was fine until she changed her number which couldn't be traced even after myriad of futile attempts.

"Hello, good morning Moksha," it wasn't Poonam for sure.

"Yes, hello. This is Rijoy. Could you please connect me to Mrs. Singha?"

"And what is this call about?"

"Well… It is something personal."

"Well…," she mused for a while. "She isn't in the office now; you may please leave your name and number along with the message with me. I will…." The call was disconnected.

"What a crazy bum. 'It's personal'…crap, what the shit personal, wasted my time, jerk." Gracy got back to work, listing down all the appointments of Poonam for the day.

Rijoy could sense his diffidence. He had to chalk out some other way to speak to Poonam. It was urgent, really urgent this time.

***

Boss had called for an urgent meeting. The delegation had proponed the visit and they wanted the presentation to be put up the very next day of their arrival. Poonam was supposed to head it. She had been working day and night on this Italian project and Rijoy was not unaware. Rijoy was doing his best to give the least of his support to Poonam and tried to obstruct her efficacy in the best possible way. He even once tried to delete the presentation from her computer, but she had saved one copy of it as she had already smelled his malefic intentions.

The meeting commenced at 10:30 am sharp. Poonam sat beside her Boss who was chairing the deal. All eyes were fixed on the screen including Rijoy's and the presentation began.

"The consolidated estimate of putting up the chemical plant will be 2.5 crores. The proposed land is away from the residential area, in the suburb but very close to the resource hub so that the cost of transportation of the raw material is categorically reduced. We have also planned to construct few annexes for the workers so that the time of commutation could also be cut down. The area will also have a running dispensary to cope with any imminent health hazard. There is also a provision of 24 hours running mess as we will have the factory workers work in two shifts that is; morning and evening. We do not wish to leave any stone unturned, Gentlemen."

Her boss's grin widened in conceit.

"The built up area will be 2225 sq yards. The bifurcation of the investment and the profit share is here gentlemen..

Investment and profit share: 40-60

Cost of installation of machinery: 1.6 crore

Building material: 2 crore...."

She looked at the figures again. 1.6 crore, 2 crore, 76 lakhs... The figures were incorrect. How could this happen, she had checked the entire presentation the last night.

The boss's eyes were burning holes in her confidence. It was a blunder and the clients were really important.

The deal was vital. Beads of indignation swept her confidence down on the floor; she was sweating profusely.

"Sir, I have my figures correct. May I please take the presentation forward?" Rijoy's voice echoed in the room.

After the nod of approval from the Boss, Rijoy gave an immaculate presentation with all the figures correct; sounding the bugle of triumph over Poonam, his team head and his wife.

So, Rijoy fiddled with the figures. Poonam thought aside.

To honour his victory Poonam resigned from the job and after a fortnight she found that she was pregnant with Rijoy's baby.

Rijoy, who had tricked her- his baby.

***

Rijoy would have to trick Poonam again, but only this time to give her the correct figures of Sayra's life.

Chapter 6

Amol was tracking the flight schedule. How desperately he wanted a return ticket to India and more importantly return to Sayra who he needed the most.

"It's a chalk a blocked schedule for another two days," said the ticketing executive.

Please understand the exigency. I have to reach India at the earliest.

I am sorry Sir,...but wait just one ticket is available for Wednesday March 4, which will be over morrow.

March 4, the eve of Sayra's birthday.

Sir, there is a long queue waiting behind you. Please take a quick decision. Yes or no?

Yes, yes. Please book me on the flight.

That will be $820. Card or cash?

Cash.

***

Poonam was in a meeting when Gracy called.

I told you Gracy not to disturb me. I am in the middle of a very important meeting.

Madam, the Sterling Road storehouse is on fire, a cop is online.

"Excuse me gentlemen," she turned to the German delegates and rushed with the cordless out of the office.

"Connect the phone, hurry up connect the phone."

"Yes, madam."

"Hello this is Poonam," she was running out of breath.

"Poonam... This is Rijoy."

Rijoy...this can't be her Rijoy, he had never ever called up. So, why will he call up now? It was the cop, the cop Rijoy.

"Yes Sir. Please tell me how bad is it?" The pounding of her heart could be heard across the line.

"Poonam, it's about our daughter, our daughter Sayra and it is really bad."

Poonam found her body sinking to the ground, weighed down by both by the news and Rijoy's voice. It was her Rijoy, finally he had called...called but what for what? To give a piece of news that her ears were not ready to take!

"When can I see you Poonam?"

"As soon as possible Rijoy, as soon as possible. I am at my Nirvana Road office and will be waiting for you."

"I am right outside your office Poonam."

Rijoy found himself seated in a huge cabin furnished in mahogany and straight across him was sitting his

Poonam, still vivacious. Not a wrinkle had marred her face, but it wasn't the time to admire her beauty.

"Rijoy-Poonam!"

Their names resounded in their ears; elicited out in concurrence with each other.

"What happened to Sayra? She got married didn't she? Please say something Rijoy, my soul can't take another blow. Say something please."

"Sayra met with an accident, she is in coma. She needs us. She needs her parents. Poonam she needs you and me. Our daughter needs a miracle!"

"She is paying for my sins. I am sorry Poonam, its coming back to me. I am sorry…really sorry Poonam."

Rijoy narrated her entire story and tried to bridge gaps; those gaps which could never be bridged.

Poonam could not contain herself any longer and her heavy steps and depressed soul took her closer to Rijoy. Her arms wrapped around Rijoy's shattered spirit instantaneously and they both sobbed hysterically like children. And with the tears they purged out their egos, their grievances, their ephemeral hatred, their embedded wrath and out came their love and concern for each other. Their apologetic eyes glistened red with love, guilt, repentance and worry for their daughter.

They found love for each other back and now they had to find a miracle.

***

Sayra looked more beautiful than her profile pictures on the social media, even when she was pale complexioned with the masterwork of bruises all over her body. Poonam ran her fingers through her tangled hair, her broad forehead, her big eyes, her sharp nose and her full shaped lips- Rijoy's lips. She was 7 when Poonam had to leave her and move ahead in life. She didn't desire so, but was compelled by the law to leave a piece of her heart and soul with Rijoy.

Time has changed, Sayra has changed and Rijoy, yes he too has changed. **Changed for good**.

***

She travelled back to her somber past…

Poonam was apprehensive about Rijoy's response when she disclosed the news of her pregnancy to him. She had well prepared herself that if he asked her to abort the baby; she would rather abort their marriage and go back to her father's house.

"Poonam, Poonam, Poonam, I can't tell you how happy you have made me." He swirled her around lifting her in his strong muscular arms.

It wasn't a dream, he was really happy. She had seen him smiling wholeheartedly after a very long time. Yes, he was happy this time.

"You shouldn't exert yourself much now, I will call for a domestic help to your aid. Absolute rest from now on."

"Rijoy, it's alright I can manage without a help; the finances are…" She chose to remain silent for she knew that Rijoy would not like hearing about finances which was his sole onus now.

Rijoy's smile had left his face.

"I mean that I don't want a 24 hours help as that will intrude our privacy, let's hire someone who would come at 9 in the morning and leave at 6 in the evening."

The motion was carried forward this time and Divija joined not merely as a help but a comforting pillow to Poonam to who she could speak her heart out, cry out her frustration, make her a punch bag and hug her with all the warmth.

Chapter 7

Divija was a medium heighted and dark complexioned meticulous lady. She divorced her husband at the age of 24; the age when people usually get married. The alimony granted to her by her husband was a sum of 5,000 INR, a malnourished boy of 8, few broken teeth and a fractured arm. She accepted it all with grace, dignity and happiness. It wasn't an easy decision for her to take but she surfaced up as a headstrong female who was the owner of her life and slave of none. She was subjected to taunts and jibes of the society; belonging to the lower section of the community she was ostracized for taking such a bold step and thereafter she started working as a domestic help, renting a small and peaceful quarter for her son and herself.

Divija was the testimony to Poonam's pathos. Rijoy took full care of her physical health but, she was suffering mentally because his male ego was crushing her day by day.

"What's the matter Rijoy? Your pallor speaks for your worries. Are you tensed about something?" Poonam ran her fingers through his curly hair showing her concern.

"It's just this silly client who is expecting bizarre things out of the project and the Boss is turning equally eccentric, driving us all crazy. Look at the project, how immaculate it is, absolutely picture perfect. Now what is he trying to do? Open up a can of worms?" He pointed at the draft on the monitor.

Poonam ran her eyes through the draft. There was an erroneous blunder, she at once leaped onto her feet to do the necessary amends; she had mastered working on such projects.

"Rij, the client is correct. See, here is the error." She pointed out her long enthusiastic finger towards the screen.

But, her Rij felt that the accusing finger was pointing out at his incompetency. And his face changed colours from pale yellow to red and then to purple. Poonam sensed it.

"Really Poonam? So, yet again you have proved that I appear to be a moron to you, no brains and no knowledge, super inefficient. For God's sake! When will you stop being my boss? Or have you really forgotten how I saved the skin of the company when you fumbled with the figures in front of the client?"

Figures… Yes Rijoy had changed the figures to earn the credit and show her down. How could she forget that afternoon when he had stabbed her in her back. This very recollection of betrayal by her love brought tears in her eyes *and she started sobbing like a child.* Her child inside her womb was at unrest to feel her sobs.

Rijoy looked at her and then at her bulging belly which showed signs of movements of the life growing in her; he melted down.

"Poonam, why do you do this? See, what you have done to the baby… Comm'on stop crying now." He wiped her tears and held her closer to him to pacify her.

Poonam knew that Rijoy was less concerned about her and more about the baby. She had again learned a lesson to not to rectify his mistakes. But she was vexed as Rijoy's performance at the office was on a decline.

Her opinions on the official matters stood worthless in spite of her prowess. Rijoy didn't like her giving him any advice as he did not wish Poonam to supersede him. Her talent could not stand firm on Rijoy's grounds of self pride and patriarchal conceit. Days passed and then months when finally the day arrived…

"Sahab, Madam is in pain; the labour pains have begun. She needs to be taken to the hospital immediately." Divija was panting on the phone.

"Divija, I will call for an ambulance. You please be at her side. Make sure that nothing happens to the baby and Poonam. I will be there in another 45 minutes."

Poonam delivered a beautiful and healthy baby girl on March 5, 1994. She was fairer than the snow, prettier than life sprouting out on a barren land, her eyes brighter that the sun and her hair were black gold. She was Rijoy's reflection of his love for Poonam. He named her Sayra.

Chapter 8

Sayra was Rijoy's treasure, his life, his part of soul and so was she for Poonam. He made sure that Poonam had no other job except for attending to Sayra's needs and hence Divija stayed. He had also changed his job and joined an organization where not much of his analytical skills were required and he flourished. Also, flourished his disputes with Poonam. But this time it wasn't an uncalled for professional guidance from her side; it was parenting.

Rijoy started finding faults in Poonam and blamed her even if Sayra was under the weather. He accused her for not taking care of Sayra properly. He thought that Poonam is taking revenge on Rijoy by not taking good care of Sayra. **Divija was watching everything.**

Rijoy's love for Poonam had not grown less during these years but his insecurities were growing more. Initially, it was professional insecurity and now it was Sayra's upbringing. He had lost his parents at a very young age and now it was Sayra who was his blood hence, this state of paranoia. Divija felt sorry for Poonam and time and again stood in her support. She had become Poonam's succor, her pillar of strength. Their conflicts grew as Sayra grew up. But, Sayra continued to be her father's heart and mother's soul.

She took her first step when she was 10 months old and Rijoy was on cloud 9 that day. She spoke the first word when she was 11 months; it was "Dadda." Rijoy threw a party at his office. He was the best dad in the world. He got Sayra new dresses, toys and now their house smelled of all sorts of baby products. She was her princess but unfortunately he could not treat the mother of his princess as a queen. Their differences had widened up and in the deep chasm was buried their love for each other.

Poonam's parents paid them a visit once in a blue moon as Rijoy did not like their interference much in his life.

It was Sayra's first birthday and they had planned to celebrate it in an orphanage to share the happiness with the less happy ones; Rijoy knew how it felt to be an orphan. Sayra was wearing an onion pink frilled frock brought by her father and looked no less than a cherub. Rijoy was waiting outside in the car for Poonam, Sayra, Divija and Poonam's parents. Sayra wet her dress and Poonam made her change into the yellow frock brought by her parents. The moment Rijoy saw Sayra not clad into her fairy dress and into the dress brought by his in-laws he felt defeated. He did not speak a single word until her parents left. The rest of Sayra's first birthday was spent in arguments and quarrels ending into a few physical blows presented to Poonam as a return gift. **Divija was watching.**

The next day, Divija for the very first time advised Poonam to abandon such a relationship full of agony and wrath. Poonam did not respond to her advice but later that evening when again Rijoy misbehaved, she packed her bags and left for her parent's place with Sayra.

Rijoy found it difficult to sleep without his daughter and yes…without his wife. The next day, Divija as usual made breakfast for him which kept on embellishing the dining table even after Rijoy left. He couldn't concentrate on his work in his office and so he took a half day off from the office and headed straight to Poonam's house keeping his ego aside. He was going to see them after 24 hours and he only knew how arduous these hours were. He bought some flowers and Poonam's favourite dark chocolate to please her.

The door was open and he barged in directly only to surprise all. Poonam was exhilarated to see her husband who had come to make amends and apologize to her. So, she instantly forgave him.

Her biggest mistake!!

The next few weeks were full of surprises and jubilant celebrations for Poonam. She got her lost love back. Divija was happy too, but kept on exhorting her which was neglected as she had ingrained her trust back in her husband. Nevertheless, Divija was merely a domestic help so she continued to help her masters with utmost sincerity and loyalty.

Poonam could smell the petrichor after the first showers of rain arising out of the earth. She felt rejuvenated from within and asked Divija to take an off for the day. She cooked dinner for Rijoy and lit scented candles in the room to welcome her beloved. Her love found its roots back and so did Sayra's fever. Her body was burning like a furnace and was immediately rushed to the hospital after her father's arrival.

Rijoy lost his temper and the history repeated itself.

Their life was back on the same track. Sayra was now 5 and she had often seen her parents fighting for no reason other than clashing of their superegos or some uncanny misunderstanding. Twice or thrice Poonam fled to her parent's house with Sayra until the day when Rijoy severed all her ties with her parents and held Poonam captive in her own love nest which they had built together. **Divija was watching.**

Sayra had started going to the school but turned out to be diffident and quiet child unlike her mother. Her tender age could not handle all those disputes. However, Rijoy tried his level best to not to abuse Poonam physically in front of her and it happened only when she was fast asleep. **But, Sayra was watching.**

Poonam's life was made miserable by Rijoy, not because of any hatred; he loved her but the ego that stood superimposed over his feeling of love for her. Poonam would have committed suicide if only Divija had not been on her side; however she always overruled her suggestion of parting away from her husband. It was Sayra's seventh birthday and she had called a few of her friends along with their parents at a gaming zone. Sayra insisted on her mother going to the salon as she wanted her mother to look the most beautiful of all on her birthday and yes, the makeover brought surprising results. The party was a hit and Rijoy was full of vanity, taking the credits of organizing the party. Sayra's friend Kelvin's Dad turned out to be Poonam's childhood friend, Rishi. Poonam was really delighted to see Rishi after ages, but Rijoy wasn't. They kept themselves engaged in conversation till the last guest left. Rijoy thought that Poonam had fallen for **her** Rishi.

"How can you even accuse me on this? My goodness! What a pervert you are!"

She felt his fingers burning in fury hard on her face and then he pushed her on the bed.

"So, you really want to see what a big time pervert am I?" He unzipped his pants and pushed himself into her, "and this was what you probably wanted."

She was raped.

Sayra was not watching, Divija was!

Rijoy was a victim of a misunderstanding which was going to ruin his family and his entire life.

He did not stop here; he ripped apart the dress that Poonam had worn that day and burnt it to ashes. He was about to charge again at her when Divija came to her rescue. This time Divija hit him hard across his face leaving him baffled. She knew how to take the bull by the horns and she did.

Poonam knew that she could take no more of this shit, she had to take a decision and if it wasn't now then it would have had been never. Divija helped Poonam pack her baggage.

"Syara is not going along with you." He lifted Sayra from the bed and held her closer to him. "You go wherever you wish to, but not definitely her, she is my blood."

"Rijoy, you are insane, you will ruin her future too and she will hate you for this." She sobbed, "and if this is your wish then let your wish be granted." She knew how rampageous and dangerous Rijoy could turn but, she also knew that he loved Sayra more than anything or anyone else in the world. Hence, it was better to leave otherwise these disputes would have ended up costing Sayra's happiness forever.

Sayra was awake by then and was equally sobbing as her mother.

"Remember, I won't ever let you come in Sayra's or my life back. It's over." His sagaciousness told him that Poonam will return to her family in few days; he was wrong.

Sayra cried out "Mumma…" And Poonam was gone.

****

Sayra cried out "Mumma…" And she woke up from the deep slumber only to find her head resting in her mother's lap and her father standing beside her mother as an unstinting support. It was March 5, 2016. Her birthday on the hospital bed; she was happy still!

Chapter 9

She couldn't believe whether she was out of coma and hallucinating or was still in coma and dreaming of this utopia. She closed her eyes and opened again and then closed and then repeated till her mother called out her name, "Sayra."

She still hasn't changed. She looked as beautiful as morning dew with few silver strands complementing her peach-golden complexion, her lips curved in a warm welcome and her eyes- those big green eyes; glittering with tears of love and separation. Her dad…her dad looked worn out but. She was meeting her dad after two long years. Amol had forbidden her from meeting her dad and now she will forbid this relationship without any repentance; she was united with her family.

She wanted to die few weeks back; now the desire of living with her mum and dad together glistened in her eyes and her parents could read it.

"Good morning, beautiful girl. How are we feeling now? I was told that you slept for almost 2 weeks. Not bad…hope you feel fresh now," smiled the Head Neurosurgeon who was called especially from London to perform surgery on Sayra. It was a traumatic brain injury which brought along with it blood clotting and swelling. The case was critical!

Poonam kept looking at her precious daughter. The doctor looked familiar and Rijoy did not take long to recognize him.

"Poonam…is that you Poonam? Poonam Singha? My god! You haven't changed at all," said Rishi, her childhood friend and the Head Neurosurgeon.

Poonam could only manage a faint smile and looked at Rijoy who was smiling back at her. Yes, it was the most genuine and understanding smile she had ever seen on his face, he wasn't suspicious.

"Rishi, you have come as a blessing in disguise. Poonam and I are so happy to see you to have come to our daughter's rescue."

"Oh! Mr. Singha. Sorry, I didn't notice you. Don't worry things will fall in place eventually. I would like to have a look at her reports, so that we can schedule the operation as soon as possible." He started studying the reports in a pensive mood.

"Sayra, you are a brave girl and I am sure you will fight out this diminutive clot. Mr. Singha, can I have a talk aside moment with you please?"

"How bad is it?" Rijoy knew the truth already, he had raided many doctors' knowledge and proficiency before Rishi arrived.

Rishi wasn't expecting such a direct question. "It's bad, really bad. The risk factor is higher. But we anyways have to take a chance. If we don't go for an operation soon then seizures will soon take over her entire body and the things will worsen day by day. She might again go under coma and never recover. I don't want to threaten you but Rijoy, it's fatal." He placed his sympathetic hand on Rijoy's shoulder and patted.

"When at the earliest can the operation be scheduled?" He was already trembling.

"We will fix on a date in a day or two and inform you. Take care of yourself and Poonam, both of you need to be strong, really strong."

When Rijoy returned to the cubicle where rested his princess and the queen of his heart, he sensed the tension in the air. Sayra was peacefully asleep but Poonam... Poonam was waiting to hear from Rijoy.

This time they did not speak to each other because their eyes did the talking and they hugged each other tight and wept...wept through the noon. They wept on their daughter's state, their family reunion, the time that would never come back, the moments of love and compassion that they deliberately ostracized from their lives...and hundred other reasons to weep for. Even the tears could not shed off the burden they carried in their hearts...the burden of guilt.

Sayra watched them through the parted curtain of her eyes but did not weep, finally she could experience in life what she longed for; not her father's and not only her mother's but her parents' love. That day they had their lunch together. They feasted on love and forgiveness.

They had learnt a lesson in life... But it was too late... too late.

***

Something was still bothering Sayra. It was her love, her love for Amol and his betrayal. These thoughts struck her time and again and did not let her enjoy completely the eternal love of her parents. Only and only if she could delete that date…the day of her 17th birthday from the novel of her life…

Chapter 10

Sayra was going to turn 17 in the next few minutes. The clock struck half past eleven. Amol had planned a midnight birthday bash for just the two of them.

She was not waiting for her birthday more than she was for her love-Amol. She was looking like the Goddess of beauty dressed in onion pink chiffon blouse and a pleated mauve knee length skirt- her two most favourite colours which complimented her rose pink complexion and ruby red lips. She wore no jewels, for Amol had once told her that the magnificence of her beauty outshines the resplendence of the most lustrous diamonds. So, she ornamented herself with a smile on her full shaped lips and love for Amol in her eyes waiting in desperation for him to climb up the window through the balcony and embrace her in his arms.

At fifteen minutes to 12 Amol made his way to her room and saw Sayra lost in the portrait of two lovers hung on the opposite wall. He wrapped his arms around her to not only surprise her but make her blush in the colours of his youth. She turned to look at Amol who could not help himself from gazing at her bewitching beauty, as if she was a conjurer and he was under her spell.

She jerked Amol away feeling the hardening of his male ego pressing against her soft demeanor. Amol came back to his senses. He gifted her, a beautiful watch which looked as elegant as her and insisted her on wearing the watch. But, she declined his wish gracefully; not because she loved Amol any less but

"I don't wish to be governed by time," she said planting a gentle kiss accidently on his lips and brushing her softness against Amol's strong, muscular chest. Amol was aroused by the delicate touch and he could feel the throbbing in his lions. He returned her kiss like a hungry wild beast ready to pounce upon his prey. She pushed him back regaining her senses.

Sayra, I love you, I have never loved you more than today...

Amol, it's wrong.

Let's make it a special birthday, it's just a kiss...come here

And he pulled her closer to him. Before Sayra could react any further his mouth was over hers trying to explore the sweetness of her taste. Sayra gave in to his insatiable desire by kissing him back with the same passion as that of his but like a docile deer. Her tongue explored the intensity of his desire to make love to her. He reached for her softness beneath her blouse and pressed them a little. Sayra flinched in sweet pain of desire. Amol's tongue moved down towards her lovely, firm breasts forming circles around her nipples. He gently stroked them and his tongue and teeth teased her erection, she was under high dose of ecstasy wanting to be loved and caressed more.

Sayra fell down on the bed in a swoon. Amol's hands moved towards the wet, velvet heaven on her body and his finger started stroking and discovering the unseen and unfelt beauty of hers. She moaned in pleasure and pain as he slowly drifted his mouth from her soft, firm breasts to the unexplored areas of love. He now unzipped his pants and made her feel his male hardness. It was a nine inch monster; he shoved it in the creamed cave waiting to be explored, licking the sweet smelling elixir that came gushing out in all colours of red. She groaned in pain more than in pleasure, she felt as if something was cutting through her. She opened her eyes; it was Amol, her Amol who was making passionate love to her. Now, she moaned more in pleasure and less in pain, her body dancing to the rhythm of Amol's body. Both of them in each other's embrace soared high in the passionate world of intense love making. The male energy filled her lone spaces as well as her heart, Amol shuddered giving a loud groan next to the lovely and complete Sayra.

The whole night was spent sleeping in each other's arms of love and promise. Sayra woke up to a new dawn of her life, she felt beautiful because she was happy and now was confident of him.

Chapter 11

I belong to an age where I used to write letters to my love
Furtively enough, scared of being revealed to the world…
Where I used to climb up upon the cherry blossom tree to hide my blush…
I belong to an age whence love happened for once and lasted for an eternity…
I belong to an age where science did not ruin my innocence,
Where fantasy was a place that existed,
Where imaginations soared high and rains brought not only love but song,
Where the trees sang and the birds romanced…
I belong to an age where I was you and you were in me…

Treasuring these lines in her secret diary she smiled to herself. Her fate was now smiling upon her and showering all the choicest blessings.

"Sayra… Sayra," Amol curled up on the bed, stretched his arms towards the precious morning dew which had fallen on him the previous night, "come here sugar."

"Amol, it's already daybreak. Please rush out of here before Papa discovers us together," she panicked realizing the need of the hour.

It was 5:30 in the morning and Papa would come in any time to wish her on her birthday. She rushed Amol out of the window and he almost landed in a crash. He rose to his feet, gave a flying kiss to his lady love and walked towards his den.

The door behind her flung open. It was her Papa holding her favourite cheese cake in one hand and her favourite tulips in the other. This is called a perfectly timed entry. Her father knew exactly how to make her feel special on her birthdays, but this time it was Amol who had struck a chord in her heart, resonating more than ever before.

"Daddy's girl has turned 17 today…come here give your Daddy a hug."

"Oh Papa… I love you to the moon and back."

"Love you too my darling."

Rijoy could sense the change in her…probably she was growing up.

"This will be the final year of your school now Sayra and we will have to make plans for your life ahead."

"Sure, Papa." But she had already made her plans. "Also, honey if you have forgotten tomorrow happens to be your Mathematics Exam. And, so we are celebrating your birthday in a subtle manner…just the two of us. Does that sound alright to you hon?"

She was hardly listening. She had wandered away by then to her fantasy land…*just the two of us*…her mind was again overpowered by Amol.

"Sayra... It is alright for you?"

"Sounds fun Papa...it's going to be a special one."

"Will see you at the breakfast, Sayra."

"Love you, Papa." She gently kissed her father's cheek at closed the door behind her.

Now it was Sayra, fragrance of her Amol, the messed up bed – the testimony of their love, the painting of the two lovers on the wall, the treasured gift given to her by Amol and next to it on the table was her...most dreaded Mathematics book.

Oh! The Mathematics book!!

The Mathematics Exam!!!!!

Amidst the excitement of her 17th birthday and her deflowering ceremony she had almost forgotten that her XII exams were going on and it was the mad month of March and not the spring- the season of love.

She was transported to reality.

She dashed into the bathroom and brushed her teeth, although she didn't want to lose the dominant taste of Amol's love. She bathed herself unwillingly, washing away Amol's treasured touch. She slipped into her floral cotton pajamas and a turquoise turtle neck top. However she dressed, whatever she wore, she always managed to look divine and carelessly beautiful. Yes, she was carelessly beautiful absolutely oblivious of her looks.

The textbook of problems wanted itself to be solved by the Diva and hence the wish was granted. Sayra was now lost into integration, differentiation, probability factor, algebra, calculus etc. She was so engrossed into the subject that she forgot that she had a stomach too.

"Sayra, I thought of enjoying waffles with maple syrup and freshly brewed coffee in your room. Would you mind giving me a company?"

"Oh thanks, Papa," and they enjoyed eating together in each other's company. The father and his most beautiful daughter.

Her father had spoiled her and always kernelled her inside his armoured shell of love and protection, after all he had taken parenting Sayra without Poonam as a challenge and it was undisputed success so far. But he missed Poonam…yes, he dearly missed her but, his male self was not ready to accept his longing for her. His obscured love for Poonam did not let him remarry and give another woman her place. But Poonam was not worth his male ego.

Chapter 12

Poonam, like every year went to The Christ Orphanage to celebrate Sayra's birthday. She never tried to search her daughter in any of them for she knew that Sayra was unique. Sayra- her daughter, Poonam and Rijoy's daughter. If only Rijoy knew how to love and respect his wife, they would have been a happy family together in the whole world. But as luck would have it, they were far apart from each other and all that Poonam could do to treasure them as a part of her life was to trace their existence through their social accounts through internet. Yes, internet was a boon for her. It had miraculously brought her family close to her virtually.

"Aunty, is it a cheese cake again?" said Tina the tiniest and naughtiest of all.

Poonam gave a hearty laugh at her innocent question and nodded in an affirmative reply.

"I told you na aunty that I like dark chocolate cake with lots and lots and lots of cherries on it and lots and lots and lots of candles on it." Said the seven year old. Poonam placed her soft and graceful hand over Tina's eyes. "Hocus Pocus and here comes Tina's delight, a dark chocolate cake with lots and lots and lots of cherries and candles on it." She produced a cake to surprise Tina; for she shared her birthday with Sayra and that made her special.

"Did I tell you that I love you 2, 3, 5, 8, 10."

"And so does your Poonam aunty."

Poonam reveled in coming down to this orphanage to celebrate every occasion. Coming here felt like coming to a family home to her for they all had one thing in common...**no family**.

It was a tiring day for Poonam. She attended three meetings back to back and cancelled one appointment, she skipped her lunch to save her time so that she could spend her evening at The Christ away from Moksha, but only on this special day.

She had nurtured Moksha as her baby. She had devoted all her lonely time to ascend the innovation and quality of the products and build upon client relation.

Moksha was not an instant success. She had toiled hard to bring it to this level of fame and moreover, it represented her liberation from self pity and domestic violence. It instilled confidence within her. Moksha started from a garage...a rented garage where she gave shape to her innovative creations.

It all began when after the divorce she used to measure the length and width of the streets in search of a job which could provide her a decent living as she refused dependence on her parents.

One fine day, in a quest to find a suitable job for herself she had to travel to another city. The rented car that she had hired from Gupta Uncle's travel service broke down on the way. She looked for help but, all in vain.

It was almost a deserted road which saw few passers-by and that too more of on foot travellers. She thought of waiting outside the car and prayed for her luck to work. Tired of standing for long in the hot sun, she took out the spare tyre from the boot of the car and sat on it. It was the most comfortable piece of furniture for her at that point of time.

It was the beginning of Moksha.

She received help after an hour but, the real help was the idea that had hit her mind by sheer serendipity. Not everyone gave a warm accord to this bizarre idea of hers to churn artistic furniture out of the very useless things of daily mundane.

Headstrong as she was, she pooled in all her savings and the money that she received as alimony to give structure to her dreams and in the rented garage was produced the most exciting piece of artistic furniture. Moksha's creatively and comfortably designed tyre sofa. She placed two tyres on top of each other and by the use of adhesive had put her creativity in place. The icing on the cake was the ornamentation- the unique piece of furniture was crowned with a comfortable cushion displaying vivid spectrum of colours.

If no one else, at least she was appeased by her creation. He first customer to value her masterpiece was her childhood friend Chandani, who not only bought the tyred sofa but also motivated Poonam to further her creations with her marketing strategy.

Chandani did her MBA in Marketing and was administering the household chores at her parent's house, still single and happy. Both of them chimed in at this idea and now Moksha had two people working for it.

Moksha grew from strength to strength and so did their friendship, until one day when Chandani got married.

Chapter 13

Chandani made sure that Moksha was noticed at every exhibition and every flea market, it was talked about by every lip and every newspaper, and it became the hottest conversation of every kitty party and every social event. She made sure that Moksha became a synonym to luxury and imagination. Yes, Moksha became a brand of the top notch. She took the same pride in marketing as Poonam did in creating.

In only 2 years Moksha had become the bread and butter for 478 employees, ranging from artisans to managers of top level. Poonam had become a proud owner of several workshops and luxuriously designed offices which she called the Green Bungalows. It had succumbed to expansion!!!

Chandani's parents valued their daughter's inclination towards Moksha but at the same time were apprehensive of her working with a divorced lady. They feared that Chandani might not receive a suitable alliance because of the same reasons. Chandani had been rejecting proposals so far, for she wanted to give Moksha some more of her time. At least there was something in her life that she loved doing and which had accepted her with both the arms stretched. Chandani was a plain looking girl of soft dark complexion who was born with the gift of rejections.

She had not many friends except for Poonam. Both of them were called antonyms together. Boys used to fall like flies for Poonam and she ignored them as flies therefore whereas no eyes winked at Chandani even once in her youth. She was approaching her thirties soon.

"Chandani, you aren't going to Moksha tomorrow and rather will be visiting a parlour."

"Why Mum?" Chandani showed no interest for she knew it was another match fixing ritual, probably the eleventh.

"The boy hails from a very good family and is an engineer by profession. He is tall, dark and handsome and both of you will look a perfect couple together, and to add on he lives in California." Chandani could sense the excitement in her mother's voice, which didn't sound new to her. This was a usual routine whenever an eligible bachelor used to come to rate her on her looks, her style, her way of walking and talking, let alone the degree that she earned for herself.

"OK Mum, so again I will be exhibited. And yes! Here I go for body decoration…change the way I look, the way I appear, my superficiality will be at test now." She was certainly vexed at the news of her forthcoming rejection parade.

"Shut up Chandani, I have almost given up on you. Why? Don't you desire to get married and have children? Why are you so apprehensive about marriage? You will be turning 30 next month and this could be the last person to have done you a favour." She was angrier now.

"This is what Poonam has done to you. She might have pulled wool over your eyes for sure. She couldn't keep up her marriage and now influencing you to be her partner in crime. Darn her."

"Mom! Stop it. Will you please? What has Poonam to do with me not getting married? Why? What's the need of cursing her? It's not because of her that I look so ugly, it's because of you..." *Oh God what did she just say? It was very unlike her.*

"Chandani!!!" her mother started sobbing. She had never expected such an answer from her daughter. Probably she was the one who was pestering her into marriage, rejections, frustrations and self pity.

"Mum, sorry I didn't mean it. I so much knew that I was good for nothing, still overburdening your shoulders. Sorry Mum." Now it was Chandani who cried her heart out.

"No Chand, it's all our fault we shouldn't be pressing you so much for marriage. You are my soul. I can't see in you in such a state. Don't worry I will call up the boy's parents and apologize."

"Mum don't do that please!" She said wiping her mom's tears, "Let's go shopping, and you buy me a new sari. We will then straight head to the parlour. You are not pressing me into anything Mom; I know you wish to see me happy always."

She phoned Poonam to inform her that she won't be coming for the day and left on a shopping spree with her mum.

She wore a crimson colored chiffon sari which complimented her makeover. She was looking pretty today, after all her mother had spent 3500 rupees to beautify her daughter. She was seated in her room all decked up for the ceremonial parade in front of the boy's parents and not to forget their prized possession- the boy himself.

The door bell rang at quarter past seven and came in the most awaited guests of the house. The boy was more handsome and cultured than expected. They were seated in the drawing room munching on the evening snacks and ginger flavoured tea. Chandani was escorted in by her mother; clad in full obeisance – head bowed and eyes down with a nervous smile ornamented on her lips.

The marriage was fixed.

Chapter 14

Poonam felt super happy for Chandani. She knew what all Chandani had to go through all her life. The more Chandani talked about Amit the more Poonam missed Rijoy, but Rijoy was a man of ego and violence so she jerked the memories aside and rejoiced in Chandani's wedding preparations.

On November 12, Chandani got married and Poonam was left alone all by herself and her sapling, Moksha, which kept her too busy. Now she had to look after the fort vacated by Chandani. She picked up well and became busier than before. So busy that she almost forgot her childhood friend, Chandani.

Chandani had savored two months of happy married life and was still not able to believe her fate. Amit was a perfect husband who any woman would gravely desire. He looked after Chandani and made sure that she felt comfortable in this alien city of California. He took her out for dinner every weekend and took her out shopping every fortnight. She felt blessed to have him as her life partner until one day, she discovered that Amit…her Amit did drug.

This discovery enraged her so much that she bombarded Amit with questions that he had never expected his wife to have known. That was the last day Amit maintained his disguise of a good husband. January 15, 1985- the day when Amit rewarded Chandani with sharp slaps on her face to honour her audacity of questioning him on drugs. This continued then on almost every day. The castle of love, trust and confidence that Chandani had once built came crashing down into rubbles and she had to live with it…but for how long, was the question.

February 23, 1985- Chandani discovered that she was two months pregnant with Amit's baby. She could not decide whether to be happy at the news of a new life that was now developing in her womb or to despise herself for bearing Amit's baby. Nonetheless, Amit was on seventh sky after hearing the news. March 31, they figured out that it's going to be a baby boy. This news brought about a great change in Amit's attitude. He was going to father a boy. The high spirited to be father now started taking good care of the mother of his son. He made sure that Chandani was in the pink of her health, both physical and mental. He had stopped doing drugs!

Few months passed. It was the season of sun in California, the month of August. The clock showed half past eleven and there was no sign of Amit. She lied down on the bed with her eyes wide open, waiting for Amit. She felt lonesome. She fell asleep.

"It shall end soon… It's a dream…no it's a nightmare," she said to herself. The universe seemed to zero down and collapse upon her and the entire room reverberated with her painful shrieks resounding with his eerie laughter. She could not believe that she was being raped…raped by her own…her own husband. He did drugs again and that day too it gripped him in its devilish clutches, he gave in to his grave evil lust and seemed to be oblivious of the very fact that he was raping his 8 months pregnant wife. He gave a loud groan and succumbed to intoxicated slumber. She kept on weeping…weeping not because of the incessant pangs of pain…but, she was scared to lose her first unborn baby. She wanted to make it to the next day… With the break of dawn her breath loosened and broke. She did not lose her baby but abandoned the world with her unborn. The next morning the bed, the walls, the room, the vicinity was mourning but not Amit, he was sleeping.

Poonam almost suffered a nervous breakdown when the news of Chandani's demise reached her. She had once again lost her family. She cursed herself for not being in constant touch with her Chandani. But what good was repenting? To keep her memory alive she named her bottle lamps after Chandani, which turned out to be another hit in the bloodline of Moksha.

Chapter 15

Sayra was fretful and apprehensive about her class XII results. She had thrown out thrice since morning and was still feeling queasy. This was the very first time she was going through such extreme result anxiety. Yes, she was scared about the Math paper; probably this was causing her bile to rise to her mouth. She had done the trigonometry and probability questions all correct, integration and differentiation might fetch her full score. She was but skeptical the most about calculus, algebra and linear programming. Good Lord! and they constituted maximum marks of the paper. She was under a dizzy spell and fainted.

She was rushed to the hospital immediately. The doctors performed several blood tests as this wasn't certainly all because of her tensed state of mind. They were trying to find all probable answers.

Before her exam results were out, her pregnancy test came positive!

She was vexed and her father perplexed. He asked the doctors to perform the test again. So, again the syringe sucked the blood out of her veins and the test was yet again positive. Rijoy instantly knew, it was Amol.

Paramjeet was Rijoy's next door neighbour and the stories of Param and his wife Sweety being the most inhuman creatures and avaricious were famous all around in the town. Amol was born to this couple who were a family friend to Rijoy which paved way for the affinity between their children. Amol had taken after his father in his looks but not in greed for money but, greed for sinister pleasure. Amol, till his childhood was the naughtiest man born on the planet and Rijoy had liked him then. He wanted to marry Sayra to him when Sayra was 9 and Amol was 13. He changed his decision when he saw- the teen Amol. Amol had become a young and carefree man in his teenage who didn't wish to waste a single minute of his boyhood.

The girlfriends of Amol changed with the season. During summers he would be spotted with a girl who was cool enough to suit his moods, a hot girl was seen comforting his winters, autumn brought along with it a girl who was open minded and spring, a colourful lass. Rijoy had spotted him out more often than less but, never discussed it with Sayra for he did not want to ruin her innocence and Sayra and Amol were friends, casual friends. Rijoy had full trust on his well protected daughter.

Sayra's beauty was not hidden from Amol, it just did not appeal him because he was always busy in other girls than her; they gave him whatever he desired and Sayra… Sayra was only a beautiful sweet friend along with who he had spent his childhood.

Rijoy made sure that she studied in an all girls' convent school and went to the coaching institute which was right in front of his house so that, nobody could take an advantage of her naïve nature but, little did he know that there was a wolf in the backyard.

Sayra was a sweet and sensitive girl who was oblivious of her beauty and that made her more beautiful. She had always fancied a love marriage and Amol to be his prince charming. She had hidden these ambers of love deep inside her heart for him since ages untold. They met everyday like close chums and discussed their daily drill. Sayra always used to listen to him and he always used to dominate the conversation, which delighted Sayra. Amol's conversation string ranged from his new gadgets to the newest of his pranks, from the new hangouts that he had visited to his newest of crushes and their gorgeous figures and candid relation.

She envied all his girlfriends and wanted to be in their place and hold on to Amol for the rest of her life, but Amol was least interested as he had always seen a friend in her; had he seen a lover in her then their friendship wouldn't have lasted this long.

Sayra nor could vent out her emotions in front of Amol as she was apprehensive of his rejection and neither could she display her ardent desire in front of her Mom; for she didn't have one. She missed her Mom so much especially on such occasions when she needed a shoulder to rest her head on or a lap to soak her tears. Rijoy knew that she missed her mom the most as he did, but his love had surrendered long back against his ego. He wanted her back but, only at the cost of her apologies.

But right now the need of the hour was not Poonam but the solution to this situation.

Chapter 16

He had loved her as a friend, as a companion, as a counselor, as a succor to his life and yes, as his wife. He always wanted her to be his last one and the special one. She had been his lucky charm from ever but, he never made advances in a fear to lose her friendship before her seventeenth birthday which had taken their lives by a storm.

"How dare you even try to touch my daughter? You rascal!" He planted a thunderous slap where his daughter had planted kisses.

"Rijoy! Have you lost your senses? What on earth has happened?" came Param to his son's rescue who would have pissed in his pants had his love not given him courage to stand tall.

"You keep away from all this; let me settle scores with him." He pushed him out of the duel which was one sided.

Amol knew that at this point of time it was impossible to give any plausible explanation to Sayra's father; so he kept quiet.

It was Sweety's intervention which later calmed Rijoy down. The matter was discussed with much furor in the house and was carried on to the streets and picked up by the grocers. It was an interesting piece of news which was licked by every lip without a newspaper.

Taking charge of the situation, a meeting was called at Rijoy's house with Amol's parents and Amol; victimizing both Amol and Sayra…his not so well protected daughter 'Sayra'. His conscience succumbed to self pity and guilt.

As per the formality protocol; a table was laid with myriad of delicacies which had lost their deliciousness to the current grave situation. On the sofa were seated Amol and his parents and opposite to them on the majestic Brazilian rosewood arm chair smoking his pipe and smoking out rings of perplexity and apprehension was sitting, the girl's dad. Sayra was ordered to sit in her room and weep on her destiny which lay undecided in the hands of both the parents.

The servant came and asked,"What will you like to have sir, tea or coffee?"

Rijoy's gaze was still penetrating through the soul of Amol and he had turned a deaf ear towards the servant. He was nervous and confident at the same time.

"Sir, what will you like to have?"

"Tea or coffee?" the air hostess shook him out of his day dream."What will you like to have sir, tea or coffee?"

He was on flight AL127 from Chicago to India. He shifted his gaze which was fixed in retrospection on the white cover of the seat to the flight attendant who was asking for his choice of beverage.

"Coffee, coffee with two cubes of brown sugar and no milk."

He had been pondering over his past since he heard of Sayra, time and again. But one question was reverberating in his mind and that was – why was he informed late... so late?

***

Sayra's operation was scheduled the next day and they were busy making preparations except for Sayra who was preparing herself for only and only Amol's timely arrival. Her heart inundated with emotions. She was unable to understand these undulating emotions which made her curse him at one time and yearn for him the very next moment.

Rijoy had gone to the nearest ATM to withdraw the required amount of cash to pay as the hospital fee, however, Rishi had waived off his fees still the sum was humongous so, he decided to take Poonam along with him; leaving Sayra sleeping peacefully on her hospital bed.

One thing that they didn't know was that she wasn't sleeping peacefully but, was at a great unrest with a huge turmoil resting in her mind and heart.

It wasn't their love but their destiny which brought them together to part away forever, before they could fathom the depth of love for each other that they bore in their hearts.

She remembered...their marriage was fixed not because their luck favoured them but the pregnancy test did.

Another support came from Param and Sweety's avaricious nature who knew that Sayra is the sole survivor of Rijoy, to who he will bequeath his entire property which was worth crores.

18th May was fixed as the date of their wedding; inviting few relatives from both the sides to witness the ceremony and gossip about the couple, let alone bless! Rijoy had always fancied a pompous and extravagant wedding function on Sayra's wedding but, all his dreams were knocked down by the blow of the news of her getting pregnant before marriage. Nevertheless, he still made the best arrangements at a five star hotel leaving no stone unturned in the arrangements.

All went well and finally the time came when Sayra had to partially abandon all her relations to head for the new bonds in her life. Rijoy controlled his tears to appear in his eyes; he wanted to pretend as a stern father who was against this marriage for he very well knew about the nature of Amol's parents. Sayra was in tears but, she had defeated the trust of her father and her heart was also pining for her mother who was watching the updates posted on the social media by Sayra's friends, of her wedding. **She blessed her**.

Chapter 17

Amol bit into his extra cheese sandwich prepared by the flight attendant and he remembered the first breakfast prepared by Sayra, after marriage. It was a fiasco! She tried her hands on traditional Indian breakfast, trying to make stuffed paranthas, cinnamon-ginger tea and haluwa, an Indian sweet dish.

The breakfast table was laid with decorative flowers, seasonal fruits, chocolate shake, coleslaw extra cheese sandwiches and pancakes, served with maple syrup.

"Sayra, are you out of your mind? Do you think your papa and I are going to eat this? Or have you prepared this only for yourself and your husband? I told you, I told you Param not to agree for the wedding."

This was her first day after her wedding. Sayra was in tears and came to her rescue, her husband.

"Mom, she must have made the stuffed paranthas for you and dad. I saw her in the kitchen, making them. Sayra, where is the breakfast that I saw you making; reading out of the recipe book?"

"Amol," she sobbed," they were burnt, in fact everything that I made was not eatable and the tea… It tasted bad, so I thought of making what I knew."

"Great! So, you knew how to make a baby but don't know how to make paranthas. Look, this is my house and my husband works day in and day out to earn a living and I will not tolerate any reckless wastage of this sort."

"Mom, but she is only 17. Give her some time, she will eventually learn."

"And you are only in college and will eventually earn. So better earn first to manage this extravagant expenditure by your wife. Just one night and you are favouring this girl who tricked you into marriage! Oh come on Amol, you still are my son." She knew how to turn the tables and this time too she had taken the charge of the situation.

Sayra was now bitterly crying. The air carried the moistness of her tears to Rijoy's house.

"Mom, it is not so. I understand you are concerned about the family, the expenses and about us. She will surely learn to cook and soon I will enroll her in some cooking classes. Don't worry Mom." Amol mollycoddled his mom and winked in assurance at his wife.

Sayra sought her mother in-law's apologies and went to her bedroom to rest and cry without eating anything. After 15 minutes, Amol entered the dark silence of the room biting into the sandwich which she had made.

"You never told me that you made such heavenly sandwiches. Have you tasted this piece of delight?"

"Stop it Amol, I really am already embarrassed."

"Hey, what makes you cry silly? Sayra, come here… promise me you are never going to cry. You know right, my parents have worked very hard to maintain this standard of living and that's the very reason of her anger."

"Yes, I know. But…never mind. Test of fires make fine steel and I will try to live up to her expectations."

"That's like my girl." He hugged her tight and his hands moved towards her belly which bore his child in the womb. He bent down to kiss his unborn and said, "You know kid, you have the most beautiful and sensible mommy and both of us are waiting to see you."

This was the first time she felt the joy of bearing her love's baby. Amol left for his engineering college and the entire day was spent happily munching on the breakfast which made her lunch and evening snack. Her in-laws had refused to try this lavish breakfast made by the newlywed and Sweety had back again taken charge of the kitchen.

Sayra was advised to abstain herself from going to the college and was enrolled as a private student. The reason given was, her health although, she was regular to her cookery classes to learn to cook what her in-laws liked. Both, Amol's parents and Sayra knew that it wasn't just health but it was the curtailment of her freedom.

Sweety left no opportunity to insult and embarrass Sayra and poor Sayra could not voice her emotions in front of her husband because he was busy making a career and she did not want to digress him from his path. He was working hard for their better future and their baby. Rijoy was much aware of her situation but did not intervene in their family matters.

Just in two months Sayra had drifted into the state of depression and started losing on her health. Paramjeet and Sweety had expected Sayra to get with her, the riches in form of dowry in abundance, but Rijoy didn't give her anything except for his blessings for a better future and this infuriated them. They wished they had spoken about the dowry to Rijoy but, the situations did not allow them to make way for their greed.

And so, was tortured mentally: the new bride. Amol was absolutely incognizant of Sayra's plight because she did not speak anything and his mother always sugarcoated her words. It seemed that the tragic life of Sayra was never going to end.

Chapter 18

Poonam and Rijoy were back and found Sayra lost in her own world in deep trance.

"Sayra," Poonam sat next to her wrapping her arms around her in a tight embrace. "How are you feeling now?"

"Mom, I want my diary. Dad, can I have my diary here in the hospital?" she ignored her mother's concern and desired for her diary…her personal diary.

Poonam gave her husband a curious glance. So, her daughter wrote a personal diary like she used to.

Sayra had left her dairy at her father's house somewhere around two years back when she last went to stay with him and last saw him before the fortunate accident which had brought her parents together.

Rijoy had kept the dairy in the safety valve of his room. He rushed to fulfill this desire of his princess, as always and brought with him her favourite cheese cake and violets to make her happy.

***

I may be far… But, I am not away
I may be sad but, not bleak
Life may be stagnant for a while but, not vapid
I may be in quandary but, not jaded

I may have gone weak in the knees but,
I shall awake to a new dawn…

…were the lines that she had written after she lost her baby. It wasn't her fault, it really wasn't. The happenings of that day rolled like a movie in her eyes.

It was the third month of her conception. The situations were the same with no change in her life's melancholy. Sweety's constant reproach and Param's unending greed made her life a synonym of purgatory. She lived two houses away from her father's house but, the distance seemed more than two miles. She saw her father less and pain and misery more. In spite of the fact, that she was going to bring their own blood into the world her in-laws seemed to exhibit apathy towards her and Amol like always was unaware.

The summers were unbearably hot as if the nature was plotting against her. She was doing all the household chores since morning right from sweeping to dusting, from washing to cooking. She felt a little uncomfortable as she had not even eaten a single morsel since morning and it was already 12 noon, with sun at the culmination of success.

"Mummy, can I wash the clothes later? I am feeling a little uneasy. I want some rest."

"Ok…but, is the lunch ready?"

"Yes, it is on the dining table."

"Do one thing, make some buttermilk for us and then go and rest."

"Ok." She was submissive and timid and Sweety used to take full advantage of her meekness.

She took out the curd from the fridge and the moment she churned it in the mixer, she felt something churning inside her as well. She shrieked in pain and collapsed. The buttermilk had spilt all around on the walls of the kitchen and the mixer blades were still rotating.

She opened her eyes on the hospital bed and saw her father sitting next to her.

Amol was unaware!

The doctor announced that she suffered a miscarriage due to dehydration, stress and malnutrition. He also advised to take good care of her, in order to save her from health impairment. Rijoy decided to bring Sayra home for few days, until recovery. Param and Sweety readily agreed to this proposition, saving them from the extra expenditure that her nursing would require.

Amol was phoned and a different version of the story was concocted; he had fallen prey to this fabrication.

"Who is Rijoy uncle to decide where my wife will stay?"

"He said, that we cannot take care of her and held us responsible for the miscarriage. What he was not trying to understand was that she is only 17 and her body was too weak to carry a child."

"Your mom is right Amol. We have done our best to take care of her. Today, she said that she would not do the household chores and your mom accepted gladly. We have compromised a lot to keep her happy and you know too that we didn't even ask for half a penny as dowry."

"I am going to bring her back and tell Mr. Singha that I can very well take care of my wife. I have married her."

Sweety realized that the situation is going out of control and immediately she pitched in before Amol left to bring the burden home.

"Amol…listen son, let her rest there for some time. She has just lost her baby; let her be near her Dad. She will probably feel much better and above all it was her decision too."

Amol was saddened at losing the baby but, at the same time was enraged to figure out Rijoy's interference and his wife's inclination towards her dad.

But, he had no time to get involved into all this. He knew what's gone is gone and will never come back. It was unfortunate that he lost the opportunity of fathering a child and got the opportunity of shaping his career at the same time. He had to leave the town for an interview which was divided into various levels, interspersed throughout the week. He left with immediate effect without informing Sayra, as he was cross with her at her decision of placing her father before her husband.

First seed of misunderstanding was sown!

Chapter 19

'Love,' you said was blind… Yes it was blind enough to see me sobbing…

She had shed off a lot of weight in spite of being on a healthy and high protein diet. The fact, that no one from her in-laws, not even Amol, had called up to enquire about her well being was tormenting her deep within. Little did she know that Amol did not call for the first two days because he was angry and the last few days because the rounds of interview used to get over at 11 or 11:30 at night and at times even on the next day and by the time his fingers reached to dial her number his mind signaled the fingers that she must have been asleep. But, little did Amol know that sleep was decades away from her eyes and her ears were yearning to hear his voice. Her eyes had dried in awaiting his arrival.

Rijoy knew his daughter's state, also he knew about the intentions of Param and Sweety, who wanted Amol to abandon this relation and get married to Swaroop Sakhuja's daughter who was ready to pay prodigious dowry for their only daughter, who used to limp because of polio in one leg. Rijoy did not allow Sayra to go back to Amol's place because he wanted his daughter to be taken home by

Amol or else his parents, as they too had willingly agreed to Rijoy's decision of taking Sayra home. All he wanted was respect for his daughter and their daughter-in-law.

The month of July marked not only the commencement of rains but also the arrival of Engineer Amol, who was now appointed as Jr. Consultant in one of the topmost MNCs of India. He wanted to announce this news to his wife first and to delight her more he carried her favourite cheese cake as a surprise. The moment he reached home, he called out for his love but was dismayed to learn that she was still at her father's place. The cheese cake went straight into the dustbin and -the furious HE, straight to his father in-law's house.

Rijoy and Sayra were eating cheese cake which Rijoy had brought to pep her spirit up. And this angered Amol more, as it reminded him of the cheese cake which embellished his waste bin now.

"Sayra!" he shouted her name out without entering the house.

"Sayra, come out with your bags packed in 10 minutes or else stay where you are, forever."

She froze at the very spot, where she was sitting. She had never ever thought that Amol would come charged with aggression to take her home. She shivered out of infirmity - both due to physical weakness and mental trauma. Rijoy had to pitch in or else Sayra would have suffered more of mental trauma.

"I am sure Amol, you must have been taught how to behave decently with your wife who has just suffered a miscarriage."

"Papa!" Sayra was aghast.

"Oh! Really so, the man who left his wife and never bothered to nuzzle about her whereabouts is trying to teach me how to behave with my wife when I have come to take her back to her own home, unlike you!"

Rijoy stood speechless! Yes, he never tried to, Amol was so right.

"Amol" she said in a feeble voice, so soft that it could have melted anyone's heart.

Amol turned back to find the weak and pale Sayra, clutching on to her rug sack, standing at the gate to leave with Amol. His heart skipped a beat to see such a condition of hers; in his heart he could feel her pathos. He took her hand and on his shoulder hanged the rug sack and headed to his home…no their home. He regretted his words which had shot out of his mouth to plunge through Sayra's heart, but now he could have done nothing except for trying to make up for it. He didn't feel sorry to have retorted to Rijoy in such an obnoxious manner; he deserved it right.

Sayra was welcomed by fake smiles and artificial words of concern, constantly reiterated by her mother-in-law. She was already saddened and this drama did not affect her much. They both headed to their room and Amol was still holding her hand.

"Sayra, why did you not inform me?"

"You could have called up Amol, I waited for your calls; but you failed my expectations."

"Oh Sayra! I can't tell you how much I wanted to speak to you but, even I was helpless."

"Really Amol? You can't imagine in what a hapless state I was in! Did you bother? No, you didn't, you really didn't."

"I do… I am sorry. I know I have offended you but the situations…the situations…"

"Leave it Amol, I have taken enough of it half an hour back and can't take any more of it. Never ever had I imagined that you are going to behave in such a way, without paying any heed to my condition. Please let me sleep now or else I will collapse."

Amol could not sleep that night, he wanted to break the good news of his appointment to Sayra but, the cheese cake adorning the waste bin jeered at him. He sat by her side and contemplated on the reason, why so much of misunderstanding cropped up between the two of them; he dearly loved her and now his heart grew remorseful looking at the skinny figure lying on the bed next to him. He promised himself to make things better now.

Days passed and then months but nothing went as planned and the situations remained the same. **The poignant saga continued.**

Chapter 20

Amol's flight was going to land in another 4 hours and he was finding it difficult to not to drift into his past and so did he.

Rijoy uncle's constant interference in their family life was making it difficult for both of them to come close to each other. They saw each other less and whenever he was back home there was always a feud to be found solution to or else, a sobbing and whining wife to welcome him on the bed. In order to avoid such adverse circumstances, he started devoting more of his time at the office and rose to high position in no less than four months. He had become the star employee of the company and because of his charm- the heartthrob of the female employees and envy of the males. He was enjoying his office but, not his married life.

One evening when he returned home he found his mother crying and his wife missing.

"Amol, I can't stand her any more now. She doesn't do any work properly and on being corrected answers back on the face. Was it for this day that we accepted her as our daughter in law? She is same as Rijoy, his replica."

"Where is she?" Amol sounded bitter.

"Where else…to her dad's house."

"Alright then, let her be there. I will call for a domestic help tomorrow to help you with the household chores. And you relax Mom; even I have had enough of this crap. Let her realize her priorities and then take a call. We are OK without her. Aren't we?"

This was what probably Sweety and Param were waiting for. That day, she was the one to have misbehaved with her and had left no other option in front of her to flee from their house and land up at her wretched father's bungalow, who didn't give anything in dowry and hence disappointed them terribly.

A few weeks had passed since then and neither of the two showed any interest in sorting things out. Amol could not control his masculinity for long and ended up sharing bed with one of his colleagues who made advances on him since the day he joined the office. He did not feel guilty even once. Sayra was now off his mind and this tradition of lovemaking continued at different guest houses and during the official company trips.

Their story had again become the talk of the town and this was worrying both Rijoy and Sayra. So, after a few months, Sayra decided to make a comeback but, this time she decided that she was going to take the plunge and will no longer be the docile and submissive fawn. She also had applied for a regular course at the college. When she stepped inside her husband's house, her in laws were disappointed to see her and moreover dismayed to hear this declaration of her of going to the college.

She was in her bedroom reading the novel written by her favourite novelist when Amol broke in. Amol and Sayra both were delighted to see each other and they could not hide their happiness which bubbled out of their hearts.

People usually miss each other when they are away but, this was a different case; they missed each other when they were close. Neither of them spoke anything but made passionate love to each other and now Amol felt guilty of betraying his love. Both of them realized that they had missed each other deeply and had masked their feelings only to fool their conscience. They were happy.

They planned a holiday; their first holiday after their marriage. The idea was presented to his parents which was gravely disliked but, superficially welcomed with brimming joy and happiness.

They went to Himachal Pradesh and amidst the snow covered mountains, the snow in their hearts melted. They found their lost love in the lap of nature, away from worries and sadness of life.

Oh!!! You look so beautiful...
No!! I m just loved by you...

They romanced, they loved, they played, they laughed, they enjoyed...they were blessed.

On their way back, Amol decided to rent an apartment and make a home away from his parents for he knew that Sayra and his mom were not getting along and he didn't want the situations to go worse, any further. She refuted the very idea at first but, later on agreed considering the conduciveness on both the ends.

When they announced it to his parents they gracefully welcomed their decision and offered help in making them settle down. Neither of them had expected this response and both were overwhelmed with regard and gratitude towards their parents, for understanding them. Rijoy was also happy with this stand of shifting to a new place- **just the two of them**.

Sweety had already chalked out the master plan…

Chapter 21

You may leave your past far behind but the past shall follow the trail...

Amol had almost forgotten his night outs with Sheena when Sayra was on a moral boosting trip at her dad's place. It wasn't a tale of yore when his lust had defeated his love. Monday morning, while sipping his refreshing coffee at his work station; teary eyed Sheena dashed unannounced and on his desk came flying a packet wrapped in a neat brown cover. The intuitive sense told Amol what the envelope carried, before it could reveal itself to him.

It read positive! There were two lines on the pregnancy testing strip. Amol's heart choked his throat and all that he could speak out was

"But!"

He had used precaution...every time they did it, he had used precaution. How could it happen? He wanted to shout out his lungs at her, probably she was trying to trick him in, probably the contraceptive failed, and probably he was dreaming, probably...

"Amol, you have ruined my life! I thought your wife was never coming back. You cheated on her and me... You asshole!"

He had to keep his calm and try not to be abrasive with her. She was creating a scene and he had to call a truce.

"Sheena…sit Sheena. Calm down. We will handle this. Both of us will. Count on me. Calm down." He made her sit on his chair.

"Don't you try to woo me now. You better give this piece of news to your wife or I shall. You used me enough when she was away and now you don't even acknowledge my presence. You thought I am a fool and will let you walk away like that. It's not a cake walk boss! You will have to purge for your sins…"

She did not let Amol speak and dashed out of his cabin, the way she had dashed in…still cursing him.

Amol went numb. He felt that the walls of his office were going to suffocate him to death. He was under mental trauma; he and Sayra had recently made up and were really happy together. He loved her and… Sheena…she was the one who had tricked him in bed and not him. She was the one who made advances on him, knowingly. That day too she asked him drop her home and deliberately took him to her bedroom. She kissed him first directing his hands to explore the curves of her body and he fell for her desire. **They had tasted blood and thereafter they feasted on meat.**

And, now she held him responsible for everything that had happened between them. He sipped his left over coffee…it tasted bitter.

That night Amol and Sayra fought for no reason and it continued for almost a week. Sayra as always was clueless.

It was next Monday, after Sheena's episode had taken place and it seemed as if his Mondays were under some curse or a black magic spell. It was Sheena again but, this time smiling.

"You know Amol, the best thing about your job is not your fat salary or you job title but your majestic cabin which turns opaque, the moment I pull on the blinds."

She pulled the blinds and her trousers down. He looked at her slim and attractive figure but soon shifted his gaze towards the framed picture of his wife, Sayra, placed on his desk.

"I was feeling horny so, I thought why not some fun… you and I have. What say?"

"You are pregnant Sheena."

"As if you care? Do you?" she winked at him. "A man like you, can better be my sex slave," she chuckled.

"Are you out of your wits? Do you know what you're saying?"

"I very well do. I guess you don't." she gave him a condescending look. "Look Amol, we know that what happened between us was just for fun and the other day, I was out of my mind; hence the melodrama. I don't intend to get into any serious relationship with you but, you know once a thief always a thief."

"I can't understand what you mean."

"Let me make it clear to you. I have aborted the baby I was carrying because it doesn't make any sense. But, I want you to satiate my physical desires; which is of course a genuine demand, for I am not blackmailing you for a good purse." She lit a cigarette which was kept on his desk and smoked it out on his face, making ring traps.

"Listen Sheena, when you know that…"

She placed her finger on his lips and made him dance to her tunes.

It became a regular affair since then. Sayra was oblivious.

One fine day, Rijoy bumped into Amol's colleague who was a friend's son and narrated the stories of Amol and Sheena, inlaid with a warning for his daughter.

As expected Rijoy was at Sayra's place and Amol was summoned home. Amol kept on negating all the allegations for he did not wish to lose Sayra. This ended up in a heated argument between both the male energies and the female energy, by default stood by her not so better half.

A decision was made; accusing Rijoy for trying to hamper their relationship, being an overprotective and suspicious father. Rijoy was forbidden to have any interaction with Sayra for the betterment of their married life.

Sayra was heartbroken and Amol confused. He did not know what he wanted out of his life. He felt guilty of shifting all the blame on Rijoy but, that was the only possible way out of saving his marriage. He felt bad for his wife because he was cheating on her and now he had forcefully severed all her ties with her dad, he was cruel to her but he was helpless too. He was not able to understand why he was doing so.

He loved his wife from the depth of his heart and soul but, there wasn't a possible explanation for this anomalous and stray behavior of his; which sought physical pleasure in girls other than his.

It began with Sheena and the list ascended with Tina, Somya, Rudranshi, Kanu… Lust had no end.

The greater the list grew, greater grew his insecurity of losing her. He dreaded in taking her out with him for the trepidation of being spotted by one of his girlfriends. He imposed too many restrictions on Sayra and her days, weeks and months were spent in the three bedroom, lavishly decorated flat.

It was an ugly Monday and a bird perched upon the elegant sofa of her large living room tweeted about the love nests of her husband.

Her doubts were given an affirmation.

Chapter 22

Sayra's operation was scheduled in next 4 hours and the police was at the door.

"Hello Sayra, you seem to look fine now."

"Yes, thank you much Cop."

"Would you mind answering some questions for us?"

"No, Sir, I don't think we must trouble her much. She will be undergoing an operation soon. So, let her stay at peace now."

"Dad, it's fine with me. I will answer you whatever you have on platter for me." She managed to pass a warm gesture.

"Alright then, so what all happened on that unfortunate day? Is your husband involved in all of this?"

"Oh no, definitely not. He was away on a business trip. He was assigned a project in Chicago, by the company he is working for. There is nothing at all to do with him. It was just an accident."

"We have done our homework, Miss. We know what your husband was involved into and we are suspecting a deliberate attempt at the cliff." He tried to press her more.

"Yes, you must have heard stories and I am not declining the fact but another fact is that, my husband loved me."

“Loved…loved is the key word- the past tense.”

“What do you intend to say officer?”

The pangs of her unsuccessful marriage were hurting her more.

“The story is, that your husband cheated on you time and again and when you were not able to take any more of it and you decided to bring your life to an end.”

He said it, he elicited the truth out and now, it was getting difficult for Sayra to breathe.

“Do you wish to file a charge against your husband Miss?”

Sayra was in tears. She could never do this to Amol. She loved him dearly and had their marriage not surrendered to the situations created by time and people, they would have embraced their love in their hearts forever. And Amol…he loved her too. He was only a little mislead and insecure, she had seen it in his eyes; not just once but on the uncountable moments of love which flashed back to her.

“Officer, you are trying to juxtapose two different situations which have nothing to do with my daughter’s accident and you must know that she is about to undergo an operation, so please stop being a torture to her.”

“Mr. Singha, I understand your concern, but we are doing our duty, Sir. Please don’t get offended. We have to press on all the hints to build on.” He tried to calm Rijoy down.

"Officer, the time of operation is nearing and I hope that you won't mind leaving us alone. You can carry on with your investigations later."

They left, leaving behind suffocation in the air.

Poonam was pained. Her hands went around Sayra to comfort her. Sayra knew that it was now time to unfold her story. Her parents deserved to know that, the cop was right.

"Maa...," and she sobbed more bitterly, flooding her mother's heart.

Poonam strengthened her grip on her to take away all misery and pain from her, but all in vain.

"Maa, I knew he was cheating on me. He went astray when many confusions and misunderstandings cropped up between us. Had I been wise enough to tackle the situations, this wouldn't have happened ever."

"Don't blame yourself child. We are equally at fault. We didn't set a perfect example in front of you. We were a broken marriage...it's our fault. Don't blame yourself Sayra, my love." And Rijoy too butted in with her. He was the one who should be blamed. Sayra was paying for his sins and Poonam had suffered too.

"Mom, he loved me, I could feel it and he still loves me. We got married too young. I lost my baby. There were hell lot of misunderstandings. He tried to make up for them, even did I...but... But I guess this was destined."

Rijoy felt his strength vaporizing away; he cursed himself for over protecting his daughter, for not letting her build on her strength, for not letting her brace herself to face the world. Yes, he was to be blamed. He took to a bench to save himself from the embarrassment of falling.

"And that day when his mother came to see me, she came with the proofs of his infidelity and held me responsible and you know what... She asked me to divorce him and set him free. Can you believe it? Can you believe it Mom? My world came crashing down, my love abode was deserted."

There was no panacea for her misery and Poonam knew it well. Sayra was speaking her heart out and she didn't stop her. Tears blinded her eyes.

"When he returned home that evening I was consumed by fury and hatred."

Sayra travelled her past, to that evening...

Chapter 23

Amol was looking naturally happy but, he wasn't accorded a happy welcome.

"Sayra… Sayra… Love, I have got a news for you…," he was singing his dialogue.

"I have got a news too Amol," she was bitter.

"Sayra… Are you fine?" The levels of his adrenaline lowered.

"Yes, I am. I couldn't have been this better. So, what's your news?" said she sharply.

He was puzzled by her tone and expression yet, he continued, "We are going to Chicago for good 6 years and probably more than that. And this project is going to change our lives forever, Sayra. We will be leaving tomorrow for Chicago for a week to finalize our search on the apartment, we are going to live in and the car that we will be driving…it will be fun Sayra and I have already got the tickets booked." He said it all in a breath.

"Not we…only you."

"Why are you behaving bizarre? What is it about?"

She smirked, "It has always been about you only, Amol…just you, I was never there in this 'we' and it always had '**you**'. You shouldn't have married me for only that mistake…that sin, before marriage,"

"Holy shit! Have you gone nuts? Where did all this come from?"

"All this comes from you and your affairs." She yelled her heart out on him.

He was dumbstruck. He did not know how that happened. He did his level best to keep it from her. What should he say now? Yes, he was wrong. He had been wrong since the day he misunderstood Sayra. But, he can't lose her at any cost; he would have to handle the situation.

"What rubbish…have you gone insane?"

"I was insane when I didn't believe on my Dad. He was right, so very right. You have been cheating on me. You had always been like that… Womanizer you were, you are and will always be. You were into girls, I was such a silly creature that I listened to all those love stories of yours and still loved you more and more, still wanted to be yours and now that when we are one; you seem to be so far away and this time, it is Sheena!"

His brain had stopped working. She knew it now finally. He has to face it, come what may.

"Sayra, I know that no woman would settle for anything of this sort, it is difficult but let me explain please."

Sayra wanted to listen but she was too infuriated to lend him her ears. "I don't think that there is much left for me to listen. Let's call our marriage off. There's nothing left between us."

He was dreading to listen to this. “Sayra listen, I love you and I have always loved you. I loved you even when I dated other girls and I love you still. I can’t live without you. Yes, I know that I lied to you when your dad brought this matter up but, only to avoid such a situation, to keep you.”

“What for Amol? You are still physically involved with another girl. What’s there for me to believe in you? You have already broken my trust. There are no legitimate grounds left for our marriage to dwell on. So what for?

“For us, Sayra, for us.”

“Us? Us that never existed?”

“It did, it did from always and will for always. Listen to me Sayra…please just for once.” He pleaded. “It all happened when you were away, Sheena was the one who made advances on me and one fine day I too was drawn in, to lust. I apologize… I was wrong.”

“And then? Mistake is only once and then follows deliberation, Amol. You have been making out with her time and again.”

“She blackmailed me into this and then yes I confess, I got addicted to this. I have no prudent explanation for this, but you know it Sayra right from boyhood, I used to lose control on myself on situations like these. It has been my weakness since ages. You know it well. But, you are my love, my true love. Everything else is only for fun. I am not emotionally involved with anyone, except for you. I can’t live without you.”

She clapped at this short speech, given by her estranged husband. “How clever of you Amol, to shift everything on me. Yes, I knew that I was not your first but, I thought that I would be your last. But, I was foolish. I mistook your lust as love and that baby who was never born forced you into this wedlock. I free you from it. You are a free bird now.”

“Sayra, I know you are angry now but think peacefully. Even you know that I love you. Don’t you? And you know it too that today in this 21st century who cares about all this? What matters is true love and my true love is you.”

“True love? How uncivilized does this sound out of your mouth! Don’t try to redefine true love; you are too uncouth to do so. What if I too get physically involved with someone and tell you that I love you truly? Would you accept it?”

“Sayra, there are couples who believe in open marriage. Getting physically involved with someone else, is no sin. It is the desire of one’s body. The way we desire for different types of clothes and food. It is genuine. When we shift to Chicago, there you will realize how the world has advanced and to what extent.”

“If this is your world then let me not be a part of it. I cannot believe that I getting physically involved with someone will not matter much to you. It is horrifying piece of fact for me.”

“Listen Sayra, it’s not about you and me it’s about the need.’

She jerked him away and ran inside to pack her bags and wrap up her love. She had received a severe blow today. She had never ever imagined in her dreams that Amol will say so? *Why did she love him? For this day to come?* She cursed herself even more.

Amol kept sitting on the couch trying to gather what couldn't be any more now, but he believed that things will be fine by the passage of time. He thought that when she would be away for some time, it will give her time to think and when he returns from Chicago, he will take her along and start everything afresh. He would give up this addiction of his, if that pains her. She loved him and he too. The only difference was of view point but, now he will live up to her expectations. There was no use in trying to convince her because after what he had proposed she would neither listen to him nor believe.

Syara had already packed her bags and was determined not to return to Amol ever. She headed towards the exit without looking at Amol. Amol did not stop her and she did not wish to stay.

She slipped into the car and raced it as fast as her blood was rushing through her veins. *How can Amol do this me? I loved him so much. This is how he had paid me back for all love, care and affection... he does not deserve me at all. I was too good for him. I left my dad for him... But now...how can I go back to my dad? I cannot share my suffering with him; he too made my mom suffer. I am not going back to him; I am going back to none.*

Her car had taken her to a mountainous track and it was pitch dark; 10:45 at night. Her will was driving her to her destiny. There came a point in her life as well as on the track where her vehicle took her into the danger unknown, away from the miseries of her life…away from Amol, away from her Dad, away from melancholy and pain. She was flying in the air, only to dash on the ground.

***

The operation was not much of a success and Sayra as per her parents' will was taken home, accompanied by Amol who had reached when Sayra was battling death in the operation theatre.

Chapter 24

Sayra was in her dream house lying on her fairytale bed coloured in all shades of onion pink and mauve, but only her skin colour did not match the shades of her pillow; for she was all ashen. She opened her eyes for one last time and saw her parents together in loving embrace, each trying to be each other's succor, giving each other the impassable strength to face the invincible. She looked at Amol and today for the first time she could see real love, yes, real love in his eyes for her. But it was too late now... too late. She didn't have much time to bathe herself in the warmth of that lovely feeling; she often found missing in their relationship. So, now she could be happy for one last time, for one last time she could smile, for she found her true love at last; be it for the last few breaths of her life.

She took one last breath and heaved out a deep sigh of separation. Rijoy and Poonam were still holding hands mourning together on the death of their angel of peace, harbinger of hope who now was reduced to a pale limp body, convulsed in self pity. Amol could not decide whether to grieve at the bereavement of such a lovely soul or exult at the liberation of a soul caught in the vicious circle of life...as he too was his culprit.

Amol took a corner; he had never felt so hapless. But now, he could only despise and curse himself.

I got married to a girl, who was as lovely as a swan
I saw her sobbing when she woke up to every dawn
I spoke to her
She chose to stay quiet
Her mornings went dim
And days turned night
She once possessed two lovely black eyes
Which were always gleaming wet, where the laughter had dried
May be I am the one who changed
May be my love for her was framed
But the lovely girl I shall always miss
She lies in the coffin now... White and pale but, still lovely shrouded in an eternal bliss
Goodbye my love... Wished I had dearly loved!

She did not meet a fairytale end because she was not His novel, because she could not fight her ill fate, because she wanted to reincarnate as HIS NOVEL...

Life is ephemeral but Memories are forever...

Prologue

Million Colours of the Sun

Her destiny which had always condoned her luck, was now smiling at her, same as-the waste bin which was overwhelmed at her response…and came flying another ball of crushed paper to add on to the elation of the bin which was used after months. Rebecca was smiling too, at her failure…she failed to fail again and this was the beginning of her real story…the story of her life which she wrote, smothered by ill fate.

‘The Girl who Failed a Million Times’, she christened her book under this name after putting too many struck off titles into the bin. This title made her travel the past… her past which was not so resplendent – the dark, gloomy, morose past.

It was the same past which had made her so strong and paved way for her rendezvous with present – the golden present, sparkling with life, colour and vibrancy.

‘~~The Girl who Failed a Million Times~~’. This was also rejected and thrown to embellish the bin.

‘Million Colours of the Sun’, was the name finally decided for her book cover.

Million Colours of the Sun